A PICNIC, HURRAH!

FRANZ BRANDENBERG

illustrated by ALIKI

Random House/New York

FOR:

Jolly
Alfred
Nell
Kate
Elizabeth
Emily
and
Judy
Bobby
Pricey
Hawley

HURRAH
for our
picnics!

CONTENTS

CHAPTER 1

"I wish we'd have a picnic,"
said Edward
to his sister, Elizabeth.
"We haven't had one
for such a long time."

"And I wish I had a mailbox,

so that I could get some mail,"

said Elizabeth.

"Mother and Father get mail.

Even you get mail.

Everyone gets mail except me."

Edward made Elizabeth a mailbox.

Elizabeth looked
into the mailbox
on Monday.
It was empty.

She looked into the
mailbox
on Tuesday.
It was empty.

She looked into the mailbox
on Wednesday, Thursday, Friday,
and Saturday.
It was empty every day.

"I never get any mail!"
said Elizabeth.

"If you want to get mail,
you have to write letters,"
said Edward.

On Sunday Elizabeth wrote letters.

On Monday Elizabeth looked

into the mailbox.

She found a letter.

It was from herself.

"I got mail!" she shouted.

"I am invited to a picnic."

On Tuesday Elizabeth

looked into the mailbox.

She found a letter.

It was from Edward.

"I got mail!" she shouted.

"I am glad Edward can come

to the picnic."

On Wednesday Elizabeth

looked into the mailbox.

She found a letter.

It was from her parents.

"I got mail!" she shouted.

"A picnic without parents

wouldn't be a picnic."

On Thursday Elizabeth looked
into the mailbox.
She found a letter.
It was from her friends
Robert and Judith.
"I got mail!" she shouted.
"Robert and Judith and their parents
will come to the picnic."

On Friday Elizabeth looked

into the mailbox.

She found a letter.

It was from Uncle Peter

and Aunt Ann.

"Uncle Peter and Aunt Ann can't

come to the picnic," she shouted.

"But at least I got mail."

On Saturday Elizabeth looked

into the mailbox.

She found a letter.

It was from Grandmother.

"I got mail!" she shouted.

"Grandmother can't come
to the picnic either.
But she invited us
to go to her house."

On Sunday Elizabeth looked
into the mailbox.
It was empty.
"I got no mail!" she shouted.
"I didn't get any either,"
said Edward.
"Neither did we,"
said their parents.
"The mailman doesn't
come on Sundays."

"It is just as well,"

said Elizabeth.

"I need a day

to answer my mail."

CHAPTER 2

"Today is the picnic, hurrah!"

exclaimed Elizabeth.

"Thank you for writing

all those letters," said Edward.

"Thank you for making

me the mailbox," said Elizabeth.

"It's our first picnic this year,"
said Mother.

"It's always nice to get together
with friends," said Father.

All day Elizabeth and Edward
planned the games.
They were going to play
catch-ball,
horse and rider,
and leapfrog.
They were going to climb trees,
hide in the bushes,
and wade in the brook.

Father went shopping.

Mother prepared
their favorite
picnic food.

Finally it was time

to go downstairs

to meet their friends.

Father carried the picnic basket.

Mother carried the casserole.

Edward carried the blanket.

Elizabeth carried the ball.

Just as they stepped outside,

it began to rain.

"Oh, no!" exclaimed Elizabeth.

"Oh, no!" shouted Edward.

"Oh, no!" said their friends

Robert and Judith.

"We have looked forward

to this picnic all week!"

said Robert's and Judith's parents.

"What are we going to do?"

asked Mother.

"We are going to have

the picnic upstairs," replied Father.

"You can't have a picnic indoors!"

said Edward.

"It's no fun to eat picnic food

at the table!" said Elizabeth.

"We were going to play catch-ball,

horse and rider,

and leapfrog," said Edward.

"We were going to climb trees,

hide in the bushes,

and wade in the brook,"

said Elizabeth.

"A picnic indoors is more fun
than no picnic at all,"
said Mother.

Father pushed
the table
against the wall.

Robert and Judith
put the chairs
on the table.

Their parents rolled up the rug.

Edward and Elizabeth

spread the blanket on the floor.

Mother handed out the paper plates.

They sat by the baskets,

and shared each other's picnic food.

When everyone was full,

Mother and Father collected

the paper plates.

Robert and Judith took

the picnic baskets and

the empty casserole

off the floor.

Their parents folded the blanket.

Edward and Elizabeth

swept the floor.

The parents drank their tea.

The children played catch-ball,

horse and rider,

and leapfrog.

They climbed trees,

hid in the bushes,

and waded in the brook.

"What else shall we play?"
asked Elizabeth.

"Let's play Musical Chairs,"
said Robert.

"We need more players for that,"
replied Edward.

"Let's play Simon Says," said Judith.

"We don't have enough players,"
replied Edward.

"The doorbell!" said Elizabeth.

"Who could it be?" asked Edward.

"Perhaps it's Grandmother,"
said Elizabeth.

"Perhaps it's Uncle Peter
and Aunt Ann,"
said Edward.

They all ran to the door.

CHAPTER 3

It was the neighbors

from downstairs.

"You are making

too much noise," they said.

"We are terribly sorry,"

said Father.

"We were having a picnic,"

said Mother.

"Our lamps were shaking,"
said the neighbors.

"We are terribly sorry," said Father.

"The children were
playing catch-ball," said Mother.

"Our furniture was trembling,"
said the neighbors.

"We are terribly sorry," said Father.

"The children were playing
horse and rider," said Mother.

"Our windows were rattling,"
said the neighbors.

"We are terribly sorry," said Father.

"The children were playing
leapfrog," said Mother.

"Our pictures were almost falling

off the walls," said the neighbors.

"We are terribly sorry," said Father.

"The children were

climbing trees," said Mother.

"We thought the building was going
to cave in," said the neighbors.

"We are terribly sorry," said Father.

"The children were hiding
in the bushes," said Mother.

"There is water

dripping from our ceiling,"

said the neighbors.

"We'll help to clean up,"

said Father.

"The children were wading

in the brook," said Mother.

"You are keeping our children awake," said the neighbors. "Ours should be in bed, too," said Father.

"Your children are just what we need,"
   said Edward.
"We need them to play Musical Chairs
   and Simon Says," said Elizabeth.
"Why don't you all join us?"
   said Father.
"Thank you, we would like that,"
   said the neighbors.
"It won't hurt the children to stay up
   a little later for once."
   They went to get their children.

The neighbors sat down
with the grown-ups.
Their children joined Elizabeth,
Edward, Judith, and Robert.
They played Musical Chairs
and Simon Says until it was
time to go home.

"This was the best picnic ever!"
said Edward.

"Let's have another one soon!"
said Elizabeth.

"Perhaps we can have the next one
out of doors," said Father.

"I hope you'll all join us again,"
said Mother.

"We will," said their friends
and neighbors.

"So let's all write letters
  to everyone we know,"
  said Elizabeth.
"Let's!" said Edward.
"The more there are on a picnic,
  the more fun it is."